C000178847

IT'S OBSCENE
TO PAINT THE
BATHROOM GREEN

JODY ELWELL GRIFFIN

Copyright © 2019 Jody Elwell Griffin.

All rights reserved. No part of this book may be used or reproduced by any means, graphic, electronic, or mechanical, including photocopying, recording, taping or by any information storage retrieval system without the written permission of the author except in the case of brief quotations embodied in critical articles and reviews.

LifeRich Publishing is a registered trademark of The Reader's Digest Association, Inc.

LifeRich Publishing books may be ordered through booksellers or by contacting:

LifeRich Publishing
1663 Liberty Drive
Bloomington, IN 47403
www.liferichpublishing.com
1 (888) 238–8637

Because of the dynamic nature of the Internet, any web addresses or links contained in this book may have changed since publication and may no longer be valid. The views expressed in this work are solely those of the author and do not necessarily reflect the views of the publisher, and the publisher hereby disclaims any responsibility for them.

Any people depicted in stock imagery provided by Getty Images are models, and such images are being used for illustrative purposes only.
Certain stock imagery © Getty Images.

ISBN: 978–1–4897–2166–2 (sc)
ISBN: 978–1–4897–2167–9 (hc)
ISBN: 978–1–4897–2168–6 (e)

Print information available on the last page.

LifeRich Publishing rev. date: 02/15/2019

Before you start this story
A warning to be seen
Grandma Bear will give a warning,
"It's obscene to paint the bathroom green"

Grandma Bear loved the pristine forest
Nature's rainbow to be seen

But all the woodland creatures knew
She loved the color green

She painted everything she could find,
The cave, the den, and all things in between.

Until that ill-fated day she chose
To paint the bathroom green.

Her paint was flying everywhere
Her legs and paws were covered
And she got some in her hair because,
She forgot where her head was at

And painted green
her pointy little hat.

She climbed upon the ladder
To paint around the crow's nest
Slinging paint with all four paws
Singing "Glory Halleluah" while
She crooned her very best.

But suddenly her ladder slipped
Sending grandma in a sprawl

Down went the paint and brushes
Spilling down and all around the bathroom stall.

It scared poor old Grandma Bear so bad
She felt nature's sudden call
Not noticing the spilled green paint
Not noticing it at all.

When down she sat and up she got
"Spilled paint" was not her thought.
She said, "Goodness, never mind!"

BUTT, the imprint of the potty
Was following her behind.

Poor Grandma didn't even have a friend
To tell her bout the potty print,
On her Shady End.

Grandma gave a warning
"It could be quite obscene
If you should somehow get the urge
To paint your bathroom green."

Now this was quite a story
The tale is BEARLY true.
I only did the telling
The believn's up to you.

The   End

This book is dedicated to the all-time lover of the color "green", Great Great Grandma Elwell. As she raised her family during some very sparse economic times, this gifted and creative woman loved to "Make something out of nothing." And yes, she loved the color green. She painted the entire kitchen, cardboard walls, dilapidated cabinets, chairs, table and even the worn out linoleum with her favorite shades of green. Though the family protested, she stuck with her favorite colors. A few expressions from the book like "Shady End" can be attributed to her. Some credit for the book has to be given to Great Grandma Jo who had a terrible paint spill while painting her bathroom green. So the "Grandmas" will pass the torch for storytelling to Great Grandkids, Lexi, Rylyn, Evelyn, Braxlyn, and Missy Poo.

About the Author

Jody Elwell Griffin has been an elementary school teacher and 4-H Leader for over 40 years and a rancher her whole life. She has dabbled with writing children's books and poetry and has now decided to pursue her love of writing. Although IT'S OBSCENE TO PAINT THE BATHROOM GREEN is her first to be published, she has also written GRANDPA WAS A COWBOY INDIAN and AIR-THIN FRIENDS

About the Illustrator

Elizabeth Smith is a Bachelor of Fine Arts graduate of Colorado State University — Pueblo. She is an artist who wanted to be a scientist. She has always loved illustrating animals with unique personalities. Since moving to the Greenhorn Valley of Colorado, she's been inspired by the wildlife that visit her home. From Mule Deer to Black-billed Magpies, she has a cast of characters living outside her windows. She is an avid birder and enjoys working for bird banding projects with an emphasis on ecological conservation. During winter days you'll find her tying flies for fly fishing in the spring, summer, and fall.

This book belongs to:

_____

Lightning Source UK Ltd.
Milton Keynes UK
UKHW052150270219
338069UK00003B/111/P